The Far Islands

By

John Buchan

British Library Cataloguing-in-Publication Data
A catalogue record for this book is available from the
British Library

John Buchan

John Buchan, first Baron Tweedsmuir of Elsfield, was born in Perth, Scotland in 1875. In his youth, his father immersed him in the history, legends and myths of Scotland, and he was an avid reader, stating some years later that John Bunyan's *The Pilgrim's Progress* was a "constant companion" to him. Buchan's education was uneven, but at the age of seventeen he obtained a scholarship to study classics at Glasgow University, where he began to write poetry. His first work, *The Essays and Apothegms of Francis Lord Bacon*, was published in 1894, and a year later he enrolled at Oxford University to study law.

In 1900, Buchan moved to London, and two years later accepted a civil service post in South Africa. In the years leading up to World War I, he worked at a publishers, and also wrote *Prester John* (1910) – which later became a school reader, translated into many languages – as well as a number of biographies. In 1915, Buchan become a war correspondent for *The Times*, and published his most well-known book, the thriller *The Thirty-Nine Steps*. After the war he became a director of the news agency Reuters.

Over the course of his life, Buchan would eventually publish some one hundred books, forty or so of which were novels, mostly wartime thrillers. In the latter part of his life he worked in politics, serving as Conservative MP for the Scottish universities and Lord High Commissioner of the Church of Scotland (1933-34). In 1935, Buchan moved to Canada, where he became the thirty-fifth Governor General of Canada. He died in 1940, aged 64.

"Lady Alice, Lady Louise,
Between the wash of the tumbling seas--"

I

When Bran the Blessed, as the story goes, followed the W white bird on the Last. Questing, knowing that return was not for him, he gave gifts to his followers. To Heliodorus he gave the gift of winning speech, and straightway the man went south to the Italian seas, and, becoming a scholar, left many descendants who sat in the high places of the Church. To Raymond he gave his steel battle-axe, and bade him go out to the warrior's path and, hew his way to a throne; which the man forthwith accomplished, and became an ancestor in the fourth degree of the first king of Scots. But to Colin, the youngest and the dearest, he gave no gift, whispering only a word in his ear and laying a finger on his eyelids. Yet Colin was satisfied, and he alone of the three, after their master's going, remained on that coast of rock and heather.

In the third generation from Colin, as our elders counted years, came one Colin the Red, who built his keep on the cliffs of Acharra and was a mighty sea-rover in his day. Five times he sailed to the rich parts of France, and a good score of times he carried his flag of three stars against the easterly vikings. A mere name in story, but a sounding piece of nomenclature well garnished with tales. A master-mind by all accounts, but cursed with a habit of fantasy; for, hearing in his old age of a land to the westward, he forthwith sailed into the sunset, and three days later was washed up, a twisted body, on one of the outer isles.

So far it is but legend, but with his grandson, Colin the Red, we fall into the safer hands of the chroniclers. To him God gave the unnumbered sorrows of story-telling, for he was a bard, cursed with a bard's fervours, and none the less a mighty warrior among his own folk. He it was who wrote the lament called "The White Waters of Usna," and the exquisite chain of romances, "Glede-red Gold and Grey Silver." His tales were told by many fires, down to our grandfathers' time, and you will find them still pounded at by the folklorists. But his airs--they are eternal. On harp and pipe they have lived through the centuries; twisted and tortured, they survive in many songbooks; and I declare that the other day I heard the most beautiful of them all murdered by a band at a German watering-place. This Colin led the wanderer's life, for he disappeared at middle-age, no one knew whither, and his return was long looked for by his people. Some thought that he became a Christian monk, the holy man living in the sea-girt isle of Cuna, who was found dead in extreme old age, kneeling on the beach, with his arms, contrary to the fashion of the Church, stretched to the westward.

As history narrowed into bonds and forms die descendants of Colin took Raden for their surname, and settled more firmly on their lands in the long peninsula of crag and inlets which runs west to the Atlantic. Under

Donald of the Isles they harried the Kings of Scots, or, on their own authority, made war on Macleans and Macranalds, till their flag of the three stars, their badge of the grey-goose feather, and their on-cry of "Cuna" were feared from Lochalsh to Can-tire. Later they made a truce with the King, and entered into the royal councils. For years they warded the western coast, and as king's lieutenants smoked out the inferior pirates of Eigg and Toronsay. A Raden was made a Lord of Sleat, another was given lands in the low country and the name Baron of Strathyre, but their honours were transitory and short as their lives. Rarely one of the house saw middle age. A bold, handsome, and stirring race, it was their fate to be cut off in the rude warfare of the times, or, if peace had them in its clutches, to man vessel and set off once more on those mad western voyages which were the weird of the family. Three of the name were found drowned on the far shore of Cana; more than one sailed straight out of the ken of mortals, One rode with the Good Lord James on the pilgrimage of the Heart of Bruce, and died by his leader's side in the Saracen battle. Long afterwards a Raden led the western men against the Cheshire archers at Flodden, and was slain himself in the steel circle around the king.

But the years brought peace and a greater wealth, and soon the cold stone tower was left solitary on the headland, and the new house of Kinlochuna rose by the green links of the stream. The family changed its faith, and an Episcopal chaplain took the place of the old mass-priest in the tutoring of the sons. Radens were in the '15 and the '45. They rose with Bute to power, and they long disputed the pride of Dundas in the northern capital. They intermarried with great English houses till the sons of the family were Scots only in name, living much abroad or in London, many of them English landowners by virtue of a mother's blood. Soon the race was of the common over-civilised type, graceful, well-mannered, with abundant good looks, but only once in a generation reverting to the rugged northern strength. Eton and Oxford had in turn displaced the family chaplain, and the house by the windy headland grew emptier and emptier save when `grouse and deer brought home its fickle masters.

II

A childish illness brought Colin to Kinlochuna when he had reached the mature age of five, and delicate health kept him there for the greater part of the next six, years. During the winter he lived in London, but from the late northern spring through all the long bright summers he lived in the great tenantless place Without company--for he was an only child. A French nurse had the charge of his doings, and when he had passed through the formality of lessons there were the long pinewoods at his disposal, the rough moor, the wonderful black holes with the rich black mud in them, and best of all the bay of Acharra, below the headland, with Cuna lying in the waves a mile to the west. At such times his father was busy elsewhere; his mother was dead; the family had few near relatives; so he passed a solitary childhood in the company of seagulls and the birds of the moor.

His time for the Leach was the afternoon. On the left as you go down through the woods from the house there runs out the great headland of Acharra, red and grey with mosses, and with a nimbus always of screaming sea-fowl. To the right runs a low beach of sand, passing into rough limestone boulders and then into the heather of the wood. This in turn is bounded by a reef of low rocks falling by gentle breaks to the water's edge. It is crowned with a tangle of heath and fern, bright at most seasons with flowers, and dwarf pine-trees straggle on its crest till one sees the meaning of its Gaelic name, "The Ragged Cock's-Comb?" This place was Colin's playground in fine weather. When it blew rain or snow from the north he dwelt indoors among dogs and books, puzzling his way through great volumes from his father's shelves. But when the mild west-wind weather fell on the sea, then he would lie on the hot sand--Amèlie the nurse reading a novel on the nearest rock--and kick his small heels as he followed his fancy. He built great sand castles to the shape of Acharra old tower, and peopled them with preposterous knights and ladies; he drew great moats and rivers for the tide to fill; he fought battles innumerable with crackling seaweed, till Amèlie, with her sharp cry of "Colin, Colin," would carry, him houseward for tea.

Two fancies remained in his mind through those boyish years. One was about the mysterious shining sea before him. In certain weathers it seemed to him a solid pathway. Cuna; the little ragged isle, ceased to block the horizon, and his own white road ran away down into the west, till suddenly it stopped and he saw no farther. He knew he ought to see more, but always at one place, just when his thoughts were pacing the white road most gallantly, there came a baffling mist to his sight, and he found himself looking at a commonplace sea with Cuna lying very real and palpable in the offing. It was a vexatious limitation, for all his dreams were about this pathway. One day in June, when the waters slept in a deep heat, he came down the sands barefoot, and lo! there was his pathway. For one moment things seemed clear, the mist had not gathered on the road, and with a cry he ran down to the tide's edge and waded in. The touch of water dispelled the illusion, and almost in tears he saw the cruel back of Cuna blotting out his own magic way.

The other fancy was about the low ridge of rocks which bounded the bay on the right. His walks had never extended beyond it, either on the sands or inland, for that way lay a steep hillside and a perilous bog. But often on the sands he had come to its foot and wondered what country lay beyond. He made many efforts to explore it, difficult efforts, for the vigilant Amèlie had first to be avoided. Once he was almost at the top when some seaweed to which he clung gave way, and he rolled back again to the soft warm sand. By-and-by he found that he knew what was beyond. A clear picture had built itself up in his brain of a mile of reefs, with sand in bars between them, and beyond all a sea-wood of alders slipping from the hill's skirts to the water's edge. This was not what he wanted in his explorations, so he stopped till one day it struck him that the westward view might reveal something beyond the hog-backed Cuna. One day, pioneering alone, he scaled the steepest heights of the seaweed and pulled his chin over the crest of the ridge. There, sure enough, was his picture--a mile of reefs and the tattered sea-wood. He turned eagerly seawards. Cuna still lay humped on the waters, but beyond it he seemed to see his shining pathway running far to a speck which might be an island. Crazy with pleasure he stared at the vision, till slowly it melted into the waves, and Cuna the inexorable once more blocked the sky-line. He climbed down, his heart in a doubt between despondency and hope.

It was the last day of such fancies, for on the morrow he had to face the new world of school.

* * * * *

At Cecil's Colin found a new life and a thousand new interests. His early delicacy had been driven away by the sea-winds of Acharra, and he was rapidly growing up a tall, strong child, straight of limb like all his house, but sinewy and alert beyond his years. He learned new, games with astonishing facility, became a fast bowler with a genius for twists, and a Rugby three-quarters full of pluck and cunning. He soon attained to the modified popularity of a private school, and, being essentially clean, strong, and healthy, found himself a mark for his juniors' worship and a favourite with masters. The homage did not spoil him, for no boy was ever less self-possessed. On the cricket-ground and the football-field he was a leader, but in private he had the nervous, sensitive manners of the would-be recluse. No one ever accused him of "side"--his polite, halting address was the same to junior and senior; and the result was that wild affection which simplicity in the great is wont to inspire. He spoke with a pure accent, in which lurked no northern trace; in a little he had forgotten all about his birthplace and his origin. His name had at first acquired for him the sobriquet of "Scottie," but the title was soon dropped from its manifest inaptness.

In his second year at Cecil's he caught a prevalent fever, and for days lay very near the brink of death. At his worst he was wildly delirious, crying ceaselessly for Acharra and the beach at Kinlochuna. But as he grew convalescent the absorption remained, and for the moment be seemed to have forgotten his southern life. He found himself playing on the sands, always with the boundary ridge before him, and the hump of Cuna rising in the sea. When dragged back to his environment by, the inquiries of Bellew, his special friend, who came to sit with him, he was so abstracted and forgetful that the good Bellew was seriously grieved. "The chap's a bit cracked, you know," he announced in hall. "Didn't known. Asked me what looter' meant when I told him about the Bayswick match, and talked about nothing but a lot of heathen Scotch names."

One dream haunted Colin throughout the days of his recovery. He was tormented with a furious thirst, poorly assuaged at long intervals by watered milk. So when he crossed the borders of dreamland his first search was always for a well. He tried the brushwood inland from the beach, but it was dry as stone. Then he climbed with difficulty the boundary ridge, and found little pools of salt water, while far on the other side gleamed the dark black bog-holes. Here was not what he sought, and he was in deep despair, till suddenly over the sea he caught a glimpse of his old path running beyond Cuna to a bank of mist. He rushed down to the tide's edge, and to his amazement found solid ground. Now was the chance for which he had long looked, and he ran happily westwards, till of a sudden the solid earth seemed to sink with him, and he was in the waters struggling. But two curious things he noted. One was that the far bank of mist seemed to open for a pinpoint of time, and he had a gleam of land. He saw nothing distinctly, only a line which was not mist and was not water. The second was that the water was fresh, and as he was drinking from this curious new fresh sea he awoke. The dream was repeated three times before he left the sick-room. Always he wakened at the same place, always he quenched his thirst in the fresh sea, but never again did the mist open for him, and show him the strange country.

From Cecil's he went to the famous school which was the tradition in his family The Head spoke to his house-master of his coming. "We are to have another Raden here," he said, "and I am glad of it, if the young one turns out to be anything like the others. There's a good deal of dry-rot among the boys just now. They are all too old for their years and too wise in the wrong way. They haven't anything like the enthusiasm in sports they had twenty years ago when I first came here. I hope this young Raden will stir them up." The house-master agreed, and when he first caught sight of Colin's slim, well-knit figure, looked into the handsome kindly eyes, and heard his curiously diffident speech, his doubts' vanished. "We have got the right stuff now," he told-himself, and the senior for whom the new boy fagged made the same comment.

From the anomalous insignificance of fagdom Cohn climbed up the School, leaving everywhere a record of honest good-nature. He was allowed to forget his cricket and football, but in return he was initiated into the mysteries of the river. Water had always been his delight, so he went through the dreary preliminaries of being coached in a tub-pair till he learned to swing steadily and get his arms quickly forward. Then came the stages of scratch fours and scratch eights, till after a long apprenticeship he was promoted to the dignity of a thwart in the Eight itself. In his last year he was Captain of Boats, a position which joins the responsibility of a Cabinet Minister to the rapturous popular applause of a successful warrior. Nor was he the least distinguished of a great band. With Colin at seven the School won the Ladies' after the closest race on record.

The Head's prophecy fell true, for Cohn was a born leader. For all his good-humour and diffidence of speech, he had a trick of shutting his teeth which all respected. As captain he was the idol of the school, and he ruled it well and justly. For the rest, he was a curious boy with none of the ordinary young enthusiasms, reserved for all his kindliness. At house "shouters" his was not the voice which led the stirring strains of "Stroke it all you know," though his position demanded it. He cared little about work, and the School-house scholar, who fancied him from his manner a devotee of things intellectual, found in Colin but an affected interest. He read a certain amount of modern poetry with considerable boredom; fiction he never opened. The truth was that he had a romance in his own brain which, Willy nilly, would play itself out, and which left him small relish for the pale second-hand inanities of art. Often, when with others he would lie in the deep meadows by the river on some hot summer's day, his fancies would take a curious colour. He adored the soft English landscape, the lush grasses, the slow streams, the ancient secular trees. But as he looked into the hazy green distance a colder air would blow on his cheek, a pungent smell of salt and pines would be for a moment in his nostrils, and he would be gazing at a line of waves on a beach, a ridge of low rocks, and a shining sea-path running out to--ah, that he could not tell! The envious Cuna would suddenly block all the vistas. He had constantly the vision before his eyes, and he strove to strain into the distance before Cuna should intervene. Once or twice he seemed almost to achieve it. He found that by keeping on the top of the low rock-ridge he could cheat Cuna by a second or two, and get a glimpse of a misty something out in the west. The vision took odd times for recurring, once or twice in lecture, once on the cricket-ground, many times in the fields of a Sunday, and once while he paddled down to the start in a Trials race. It gave him a keen pleasure: it was his private domain, where at any moment he might make some enchanting discovery.

At this time he began to spend his vacations at Kinlochuna. His father, an elderly ex-diplomat, had permanently taken up his abode there, and was rapidly settling into the easy life of the Scotch laird. Colin returned to his native place without enthusiasm. His childhood there had been full of lonely hours, and he had come to like the warm south country. He found the house full of people, for his father entertained hugely, and the talk was of sport and sport alone. As a rule, your very great athlete is bored by Scotch shooting. Long hours of tramping and crouching among heather cramp without fully exercising the body; and unless he has the love of the thing ingrained in him, the odds are that he will wish himself home. The father, in his new-found admiration for his lot, was content to face all weathers; the son found it an effort to keep pace with such vigour. He thought upon the sunlit fields and reedy watercourses with regret, and saw little in the hills but a rough waste scarred with rock and sour with mosses.

He read widely throughout these days, for his father had a taste for modern letters, and new books lay littered about the rooms. He read queer Celtic tales which he thought "sickening rot," and mild Celtic poetry which he failed to understand. Among the guests was a noted manufacturer of fiction, whom the elder Raden had met somewhere and bidden to Kinlochuna, He had heard the tale of Colin's ancestors and the sea headland of Acharra, and one day he asked the boy to show him the place, as he wished to make a story of it. Colin assented unwillingly, for he had been slow to visit this place of memories, and he did not care to make his first experiment in such company. But the gentleman would not be gainsaid, so the two scrambled through the sea-wood and climbed the low ridge which looked over the bay. The weather was mist and drizzle; Cuna had wholly hidden herself, and the bluff Acharra loomed hazy and far. Colin was oddly disappointed: this reality was a poor place compared with his fancies. His companion stroked his peaked beard, talked nonsense about Colin the Red and rhetoric about "the spirit of the misty grey, weather having entered into the old tale."

"Think," he cried; "to those old warriors beyond that bank of mist was the whole desire of life, the Golden City, the Far Islands, whatever you care to call it." Colin shivered, as if his holy places had been profaned, set down the man in his mind most unjustly as an "awful little cad," and hurried him back to the house.

Oxford received the boy with open arms, for his reputation had long preceded him. To the majority of men he was the one freshman of his year, and gossip was busy with his prospects. Nor was gossip disappointed. In his first year he rowed seven in the Eight. The next year he was captain of his college boats, and a year later the O.U.B.C. made him its president. For three years he rowed in the winning Eight, and old coaches agreed that in him the perfect seven had been found. It was he who in the famous race of 18-- caught up in the last three hundred yards the quickened stroke which gave Oxford victory. As he grew to his full strength he became a splendid figure of a man--tall, supple, deep-chested for all his elegance. His quick dark eyes and his kindly hesitating manners made people think his face extraordinarily handsome, when really it was in no way above the common. But his whole figure, as he stood in his shorts and sweater on the raft at Putney, was so full of youth and strength that people involuntarily smiled when they saw him--a smile of pleasure in so proper a piece of manhood.

Colin enjoyed life hugely at Oxford, for to one so frank and well equipped the place gave of its best. He was the most distinguished personage of his day there, but, save to school friends and the men he met officially on the river, he was little known. His diffidence and his very real exclusiveness kept him from being the centre of a host of friends. His own countrymen in the place were utterly non-plussed by him. They claimed him, eagerly as a fellow, but he had none of the ordinary characteristics of the race. There were Scots of every description around him--pale-faced Scots who worked incessantly, metaphysical Scots who talked in the Union, industrious Scots who played football. They were all men of hearty manners and many enthusiasms,--who quoted Burns and dined to the immortal bard's honour every 25th of January; who told interminable Scotch stories, and fell into fervours over national sports, dishes, drinks, and religions. To the poor Colin it was all inexplicable. At the remote house of Kinlochuna he had never heard of a Free Kirk, or a haggis. He had never read a line of Burns, Scott bored him exceedingly, and in all honesty he thought Scots games inferior to southern sports. He had no great love for the bleak country, he cared nothing for the traditions of his house, so he was promptly set down by his compatriots as "denationalised and degenerate?"

He was idle, too, during these years as far as his "schools" were concerned, but he was always very intent upon his own private business. Whenever he sat down to read, when he sprawled on the grass at river picnics, in chapel, in lecture--in short, at any moment when his body was at rest and his mind at leisure--his fancies were off on the same old path. Things had changed, however, in that country. The boyish device of a hard road running over the waters had gone, and now it was invariably a boat which he saw beached on the shingle. It differed in shape. At first it was an ugly salmoncoble, such as the fishermen used for the nets at Kinlochuna. Then it passed, by rapid transitions, through a canvas skiff which it took good watermanship to sit, a whiff, an ordinary dinghey, till at last it settled itself into a long rough boat, pointed at both ends, with oar-holes in the sides instead of row-locks. It was the devil's own business to launch it, and launch it anew he was compelled to for every journey; for though he left it bound in a little rock hollow below the ridge after landing, yet when he returned, lo! there was the clumsy thing high and dry upon the beach.

The odd point about the new venture was that Cuna had ceased to trouble him. As soon as he had pulled his first stroke the island disappeared, and nothing lay before him but the sea-fog. Yet, try as he might, he could come little nearer. The shores behind him might sink and lessen, but the impenetrable mist was still miles to the westward. Sometimes he rowed so far that the shore was a thin line upon the horizon, but when he turned the boat it seemed to ground in a second on the beach. The long laboured journey out and the instantaneous return puzzled him at first, but soon he became used to them. His one grief was the mist, which seemed to grow denser as he neared it. The sudden glimpse of land which he had got from the ridge of rock in the old boyish days was now denied him, and with the denial came a keener exultation in the quest. Somewhere in the west, he knew, must be land, and in this land a well of sweet water--for so he had interpreted his feverish dream. Sometimes, when the wind blew against him, he caught scents from it--generally the scent of pines, as on the little ridge on the shore behind him.

One day on his college barge, while he was waiting for a picnic patty to start, he seemed to get nearer than before. Out on that western sea, as he saw it, it was fresh, blowing weather, with a clear hot sky above. It was hard work rowing, for the wind was against him, and the sun scorched his forehead. The air seemed full of scents--and sounds, too, sounds of far-away surf and wind in trees. He rested for a moment on his oars and turned his head. His heart beat quickly, for there was a rift in the mist, and far through a line of sand ringed with snow-white foam.

Somebody shook him roughly,--"Come on, Colin, old man. They're all waiting for you. Do you know you've been half asleep?"

Colin rose and followed silently, with drowsy eyes. His mind was curiously excited. He had looked inside the veil of mist. Now he knew what was the land he sought.

He made the voyage often, now that the spell was broken. It was short work to launch the boat, and, whereas it had been a long pull formerly, now it needed only a few strokes to bring him to the Rim of the Mist. There was no chance of getting farther, and he scarcely tried. He was content to rest there, in a world of curious scents and sounds, till the mist drew down and he was driven back to shore.

The change in his environment troubled him little. For a man who has been an idol at the University to fall suddenly into the comparative insignificance of town is often a bitter experience; but Colin, whose thoughts were not ambitious, scarcely noticed it He found that he was less his own master than before, but he humbled himself to his new duties without complaint Many of his old friends were about him; he had plenty of acquaintances; and, being "sufficient unto himself," he was unaccustomed to ennui. Invitations showered upon him thick and fast. Match-making mothers, knowing his birth and his father's income, and reflecting that he was the only child of his house, desired him as a son-in-law. He was bidden welcome everywhere, and the young girls, for whose sake he was thus courted, found in him an attractive mystery. The tall good-looking athlete, with the kind eyes and the preposterously nervous manner, wakened their maidenly sympathies. As they danced with him or sat next to him at dinner, they talked fervently of Oxford, of the north, of the army, of his friends. "Stupid, but nice, my dear," was Lady Afflint's comment; and Miss Clarissa Herapath, the beauty of the year, declared to her friends that he was a "dear boy, but so awkward." He was always forgetful, and ever apologetic; and when he forgot the Shandwicks' theatre-party, the Herapaths' dance, and at least a dozen minor matters, he began to acquire the reputation of a cynic and a recluse.

"You're a queer chap, Col," Lieutenant Bellew said in expostulation.

Colin shrugged his shoulders; he was used to the description.

"Do you know that Clara Herapath was trying all she knew to please you this afternoon, and you looked as if you weren't listening? Most men would have given their ears to be in your place."

"I'm awfully sorry, but I thought I was very polite to her."

"And why weren't you at the Marshams' garden-party?"

"Oh, I went to polo with Collinson and another man. And, I say, old chap, I'm not coming to the Logans tomorrow. I've got a fence on with Adair at the school."

Little Bellew, who was a tremendous mirror of fashion and chevalier in general, looked up curiously at his tall friend.

"Why don't you like the women, Col, when they're so fond of you?"

"They aren't," said Colin, hotly, "and I don't dislike 'em. But, Lord! they bore me. I might be doing twenty things when I talk nonsense to one of 'em for an hour. I come back as stupid as an owl, and besides there's heaps of things better sport."

The truth was that, while among men he was a leader and at his ease, among women his psychic balance was so oddly upset that he grew nervous and returned unhappy. The boat on the beach, ready in general to appear at the slightest call, would delay long after such experiences, and its place would be taken by some woman's face for which he cared not a straw. For the boat, on the other hand, he cared a very great deal. In all his frank wholesome existence there was this enchanting background, this pleasure-garden which he cherished more than anything in life. He had come of late to look at it with somewhat different eyes. The eager desire to search behind the mist was ever with him, but now he had also some curiosity about the details of the picture.

As he pulled out to the Rim of the Mist sounds seemed to shape themselves on his lips, which by-and-by grew into actual words in his memory. He wrote them down in scraps, and after some sorting they seemed to him a kind of Latin. He remembered a college friend of his, one Medway, now reading for the Bar, who had been the foremost scholar of his acquaintance; so with the scrap of paper in his pocket he climbed one evening to Medway's rooms in the temple.

The man read the words curiously, and puzzled for a bit. "What's made you take to Latin comps so late in life, Colin? It's baddish, you know, even for you. I thought they'd have licked more into you at Eton."

Colin grinned with amusement "I'll tell you about it later," he said. "Can you make out what it means?"

"It seems to be a kind of dog-Latin or monkish Latin or something of the sort," said Medway. "It reads like this:

"'_Soles occidere solent_' (that's cribbed from Catullus, and besides it's the regular monkish pun)..._qua_...then _blandula_ something. Then there's a lot of Choctaw, and then _illae insulae dilectae in quas festinant somnia animulae gaudia_. That's pretty fair rot. Hullo, by George! here's something better--_Insula pomorum insula vitae_. That's Geoffrey of Monmouth."

He made a dive to a bookcase and pulled out a battered little calf-bound duodecimo. "Here's all about your Isle of Apple-trees. Listen. 'Situate far out in the Western ocean, beyond the Utmost Islands, beyond even the little Isle of Sheep where the cairns of dead men are, lies the Island of Apple-trees where the heroes and princes of the nations live their second life.'" He closed the book and put it back. "It's the old ancient story, the Greek Hesperides, the British Avilion, and this Apple-tree Island is the northern equivalent?"

Colin sat entranced, his memory busy with a problem. Could he distinguish the scents of apple-trees among the perfumes of the Rim of the Mist. For the moment he thought he could. He was roused by Medway's voice asking the story of the writing.

"Oh, it's just some nonsense that was running in my head, so I wrote it down to see what it was."

"But you must have been reading. A new exercise for you, Colin?"

"No, I wasn't reading. Look here. You know the sort of pictures you make for yourself of places you like."

"Rather! Mine is a Devon moor with a little red shooting-box in the heart of it."

"Well, mine is different. Mine is a sort of beach with a sea and a lot of islands somewhere far out. It is a jolly place, fresh, you know, and blowing, and smells good. 'Pon my word, now I think of it, there's always been a scent of apples?"

"Sort of cider-press? Well, I must be off. You'd better come round to the club and see the telegrams about the war. You should be keen about it."

One evening, a week later, Medway met a friend called Tillotson at the club, and, being lonely, they dined together. Tillotson was a man of some note in science, a dabbler in psychology, an amateur historian, a ripe genealogist. They talked of politics and the war, of a new book, of Mrs. Runnymede, and finally of their hobbies.

"I am Writing an article," said Tillotson. "Craikes asked me to do it for the 'Monthly? It's on a nice point in psychics. I call it 'The Transmission of Fallacies,' but I do not mean the logical kind. The question is, Can a particular form of hallucination run in a family for generations. The proof must, of course, come from my genealogical studies. I maintain it can. I instance the Douglas-Ernotts, not one of whom can see straight with the left eye. That is one side. In another class of examples I take the Drapiers, who hate salt water and never go on board ship if they can help it. Then you re member the Durwards? Old Lady Balcrynie used to tell me that no one of the lot could ever stand the sight of a green frock. There's a chance for the romancer. The Manorwaters have the same madness, only their colour is red."

A vague remembrance haunted Medway's brain.

"I know a man who might give you points from his own case. Did you ever meet a chap Raden--Colin Raden?" Tillotson nodded. "Long chap--in the Guards? 'Varsity oar, and used to be a crack bowler? No, I don't know him. I know, him well by sight, and I should like to meet him tremendously--as a genealogist, of course."

"Why?" asked Medway.

"Why? Because the man's family is unique. You never hear much about them nowadays, but away up in that northwest corner of Scotland they have ruled since the days of Noah. Why, man, they were aristocrats when our Howards and Nevilles were green-grocers. I wish you would get this Raden to meet me some night."

"I am afraid there's no chance of it just-at present," said Medway, taking up an evening paper. "I see that his regiment has been ordered to the front. But remind me when he comes back, and I'll be delighted."

III

And now there began for Colin a curious divided life,--without, a constant shifting of scene, days of heat and bustle and toil,--within, a slow, tantalising, yet exquisite adventure. The Rim of the Mist was now no more the goal of his journeys, but the starting-point. Lying there, amid cool, fragrant sea-winds, his fanciful ear was subtly alert for the sounds of the dim land before him. Sleeping and waking the quest haunted him. As he flung himself on his bed the kerosene-filled air would change to an ocean freshness, the old boat would rock beneath him, and with clear eye and a boyish hope he would be waiting and watching. And then suddenly he would be back on shore, Cuna and the Acharra headland shining grey in the morning light, and with gritty mouth and sand-filled eyes he would awaken to the heat of the desert camp.

He was kept busy, for his good-humour and energy made him a willing slave, and he was ready enough for volunteer work when others were weak with heat and despair. A thirty-mile ride left him unfired; more, he followed the campaign with a sharp intelligence and found a new enthusiasm for his profession. Discomforts there might be, but the days were happy; and then--the cool land, the bright land, which was his for the thinking of it.

Soon they gave him reconnoitring work to do, and his wits were put to the trial. He came well out of the thing; and earned golden praise from the silent colonel in command. He enjoyed it as he had enjoyed a hard race on the river or a good cricket match, and when his worried companions marvelled at his zeal he stammered and grew uncomfortable. "How the deuce do you keep it up, Colin?" the major asked him. "I'm an old hand et the job, and yet I've got a temper like devilled bones. You seem as chirpy as if you were going out to fish a chalk-stream on a June morning?'

"Well, the fact is--" and Cohn pulled himself up short, knowing that he could never explain. He felt miserably that he had an unfair advantage of the others. Poor Bellew, who groaned and swore in the heat at his side, knew nothing of the Rim of the Mist. It was really rough luck on the poor beggars, and who but himself was the fortunate man?

As the days passed a curious thing happened. He found fragments of the Other world straying into his common life. The barriers of the two domains were falling, and more than once he caught himself looking at a steel-blue sea when his eyes should have found a mustard-coloured desert. One day, on a reconnoitring expedition, they stopped for a little on a hillock above a jungle of scrub, and, being hot and tired, scanned listlessly the endless yellow distances.

"I suppose yon hill is about ten miles off," said Bellew with dry lips.

Colin looked vaguely. "I should say five?'

"And what's that below it--the black patch? Stones or scrub?"

Cohn was in a day-dream. "Why do you call it black? It's blue, quite blue?'

"Rot," said the other. "It's grey-black?'

"No, it's water with the sun shining on it. It's blue, but just at the edges it's very near sea-green?"

Bellew rose excitedly. "Hullo, Col, you're seeing the mirage! And you the fittest of the lot of us! You've got the sun in your head, old man!"

"Mirage!" Colin cried in contempt. He was awake now, but the thought of confusing his own bright western sea with a mirage gave him a curious pain. For a moment he felt the gulf of separation between his two worlds, but only for a moment. As the party remounted he gave his fancies the rein, and ere he reached camp he had felt the oars in his hand and sniffed the apple-tree blossom from the distant beaches.

The major came to him after supper.

"Bellew told me you saw the mirage to-day, Colin," he said. "I expect your eyes are getting a bit bad. Better get your sand-spectacles out?"

Colin laughed. "Thanks. It's awfully good of you to bother, but I think Bellew took me up wrong. I never was fitter in my life."

By-and-by the turn came for pride to be humbled. A low desert fever took him, and though he went through the day as usual, it was with dreary lassitude; and at night, with hot hands clasped above his damp hair, he found sleep a hard goddess to conquer.

It was the normal condition of the others, so he had small cause to complain, but it worked havoc with his fancies. He had never been ill since his childish days, and this little fever meant much to one whose nature was poised on a needlepoint. He found himself confronted with a hard bare world, with the gilt rubbed from its corners. The Rim of the Mist seemed a place of vague horrors; when he reached it his soul was consumed with terror; he struggled impotently to advance; behind him Cuna and the Acharra coast seemed a place of evil dreams. Again, as in his old fever, he was tormented with a devouring thirst, but the sea beside him was not fresh, but brackish as a rock-pool. He yearned for the apple-tree beaches in front; there, he knew, were cold springs of water, the fresh smell of it was blown towards him in his nightmare.

But as the days passed and the misery for all grew more intense, an odd hope began to rise in his mind. It could not last, coolness and health were waiting near, and his reason for the hope came from the odd events at the Rim of the Mist. The haze was clearing from the foreground, the surf-lined coast seemed nearer, and though all was obscure save the milk-white sand and the foam, yet here was earnest enough for him. Once more he became cheerful; weak and light-headed he rode out again; and the major, who was recovering from sunstroke, found envy take the place of pity in his soul.

The hope was near fulfilment. One evening when the heat was changing into the cooler twilight, Colin and Bellew were sent with a small picked body to scour the foothills above the river in case of a flank attack during the night-march. It was work they had done regularly for weeks, and it is possible that precautions were relaxed. At any rate, as they turned a corner of a hill, in a sandy pass where barren rocks looked down on more barren thorn thickets, a couple of rifle shots tang out from the scarp, and above them appeared a line of dark faces and white steel. A mere handful, taken at a disadvantage, they could not hope to disperse numbers, so Colin gave the word to wheel about and return. Again shots rang out, and little Bellew had only time to catch at his friend's arm to save him from falling from the saddle.

The word of command had scarcely left Colin's mouth when a sharp pain went through his chest, and his breath seemed to catch and stop. He felt as in a condensed moment of time the heat, the desert smell, the dust in his eyes and throat, while he leaned helplessly forward on his horse's mane, Then the world vanished for him.... The 'boat was rocking under him, the oars in his, hand. He pulled and it moved, straight, arrow-like towards the forbidden shore. As if under a great wind the mist furled up and fled. Scents of pines, of apple-trees, of great fields of thyme and heather, hung about him; the sound of wind in a forest, of cool waters falling in showers, of old moorland music, came thin and faint with an exquisite clearness. A second and the boat was among the surf, its gunwale ringed with white foam, as it leaped to the still waters beyond. Clear and deep and still the water lay, and then the white beaches shelved downward, and the boat grated on the sand. He turned, every limb alert with a strange new life, crying out words which had shaped themselves on his lips and which an echo seemed to catch and answer. There was the green forest before him, the hills of peace, the cold white waters. With a passionate joy he leaped on the beach, his arms outstretched to this new earth, this light of the world, this old desire of the heart--youth, rapture, immortality.

Bellew brought the body back to camp, himself half-dead with fatigue and whimpering like a child. He almost fell from his horse, and when others took his burden from him and laid it reverently in his tent, he stood beside it, rubbing sand and sweat from his poor purblind eyes, his teeth chattering with fever. He was given something to drink, but he swallowed barely a mouthful.

"It was some d-d-damned sharpshooter," he said. "Right through the breast, and he never spoke to me again. My poor old Colt He was the best chap God ever created, and I do-don't care a dash what becomes of me now. I was at school with him, you know, you men."

"Was he killed outright?" asked the Major hoarsely.

"N-no. He lived for about five minutes. But I think the sun had got into his head or he was mad with pain, for he d-d-didn't know where he was. He kept crying out about the smell of pine-trees and heather and a lot of pure nonsense about water."

"_Et dulces reminiscitur Argos_," somebody quoted mournfully, as they went out to the desert evening.

THE END

www.ingramcontent.com/pod-product-compliance
Lightning Source LLC
Chambersburg PA
CBHW030136260626
47156CB00008B/2967